To a
Lovely Lady

WB Huelsenkamp

The Very First Christmas

The Very First Christmas

by Bill Huelsenkamp

Starbound Books™

The Very First Christmas

International Standard Book Number:
1-58736-100-0
Library of Congress Control Number:
2002110492

Published by Starbound Books™
610 East Delano Street, Suite 104,
Tucson, Arizona 85705, U.S.A.
www.starboundbooks.com

Cover illustration by Bill Huelsenkamp

The Very First Christmas

There are many things about this story that you probably will not believe. The first is that this story was told to my father by an elf by the name of Elmo. I know! I know! You don't believe in elves. You've never seen one. Well, all that I can say is that, it is very rare for one to be seen, but they do exist. Just because you have never seen one does not mean that they aren't around. Have you ever seen radio waves, or brain wave, or air? No! But you must admit that they do exist.

There will be other things in this story that you won't believe. Would you believe that in our house he was never called Santa Claus but Sandy Clause for reasons that will become obvious to you when you read the story. Would you believe that he, Sandy Clause, and Elmo the Elf decorate our Christmas tree and put the presents under it each year? No? Well, my children, my grandchildren and my great grandchildren do. They know it's true because every year on Christmas morning they see physical proof that Sandy Clause and Elmo have been to our house.

When I was growing up, on every Christmas morning there were always four things that proved to those in our house that Sandy Clause and Elmo are real.

One, are the footprints that appear every Christmas morning. They are always snowy, wet footprints; one set small and the other large, leading from the fireplace. The children have measured Mother's and Father's shoes and boots and found that the wet, snowy prints are too small for Mother and the big prints are too large for Father.

Two, are the cookies. Every Christmas Eve, we children left out two soft, chewy oatmeal cookies. On Christmas morning the cookies always had a big bite taken out of one and a small bite taken out of another.

The third item of proof, are the glasses of milk. Two

glasses of milk are always put out with the cookies. On Christmas morning one is always half drunk, the other is emptied.

The fourth and final conclusive proof is the big mirror over the fireplace. Upon the big mirror, which is above the fireplace mantel on which our stockings are hung, are these words written with a bar of soap, taken from the bathroom and left on the mantle. The mirror message reads as follows:

MERRY CHRISTMAS & HAPPY NEW YEAR FROM SANDY CLAUSE and Elmo the Elf!

On Christmas Eve, every year as soon as the sun sets, Mother and Father and all of the children go to the garage to bring in the tree. The tree was cut three days before and placed in the big galvanized tub full of water so that it would not dry out. Father picks up the tree and removes it from the water and thumps it hard three times on the garage floor to shake off the water. Each time Father thumps it, Mother says, "Not to hard or you will knock all the needles off."

"I've got to get the water off so I can shape it to fit the stand. Don't worry about the needles, this tree is still fresh."

Father cuts off the lower branches and shapes the tree trunk so it will fit in the green enamel-painted, heavy, old, cast-iron Christmas tree stand. While he is busy making the tree ready the children open the chests. There are two chests containing all the lights and decorations that the family has collected over the years. They are kept hidden away in the storage attic till the day the tree is cut and brought to the garage. As Father works on the tree, the children and Mother open the chests. Each ornament and string of lights was carefully wrapped in tissue paper on the day after New Year's when the tree was taken down the year before. Mother takes out each string of lights and tests them. If a bulb is found to have gone dead over the year in storage, it is replaced and the string is carefully rewrapped in tissue paper.

While Mother tests the lights, the children unwrap each ornament. There are cries of ooh's and ah's as each ornament is unveiled. Each and every one of the ornaments in the chests has a warm memory attached to it. There is the ornament that was on the top of Mother's and Father's first tree. There are the ones that celebrated each child's birth. There are the ones purchased or made for each Christmas past. The children then add the ornament that they bought or made for this year. When the children grow and marry they take all of their ornaments, except their birth ornaments, and put them on their first tree. When the viewing of the ornaments is completed, the children take the chests into the house. With much grunting and groaning the two chests are lifted and carried into the house. They are always carried and never allowed to scratch Mother's newly waxed kitchen floor.

Mother sweeps up the pine needles that are all over the garage floor after the thumping and branch cutting. The branches, needles and shavings are carried into the house. They will be burned in the fireplace during Christmas Day. The branches are fed into the fire, one at a time, very carefully by Father. They do not last long, the needles sizzle and pop and in a flash are gone. They are gone in a flash but they emit a fragrance that fills the whole house.

The tree is carried in and placed in the stand and the four screws are tightened. Then comes the big moment when with great effort, and a little of Father's help, the children stand the tree erect. Note. I said erect, I did not say straight.

To make the tree stand absolutely straight Father must lay face down on the floor, his upper body under the tree, his arms extended. Grasping the heavy Christmas tree stand with both hands, one on each side, he begins to rotate the tree slowly. In this way, by turning the stand and tightening and loosening the screws, the tree will become straightened. It usually takes three complete rotations in both direction before Mother is satisfied that the tree is straight and presenting its best side to both the outside world through the big picture window and the living room. Mother goes out and checks the tree from the front yard and returns, closes the door and says:

"You won't believe how cold it is out there!"

"You wouldn't believe how these pine needles are sticking me in the neck! Is the tree straight?" Father grumbles from under the tree.

"There's a hole here on the left side," Mother says walking up to the tree and tugging at the branches.

"Ouch!" yelps Father," You are standing on my leg! Is it straight?"

"Sorry! Yes, I guess that's as straight as you can get it," Mother sighs. "Here, put some water in the bowl so it stays fresh."

Father takes the pitcher of water from Mother and pours it into the bowl in the stand. He shoves the empty pitcher out to Mother and says,

"Now, can I get up from here?"

"Yes, I suppose so if that's the best you can do."

Father gets up from under the tree and stands looking at the tree. "Looks perfectly straight to me, when that limb droops you won't see that hole." He goes to the kitchen and pours a cup of coffee.

"It leans to the left," Mother says.

"The whole house leans to the left," says Father returning with his coffee.

"It does not! Does anyone want hot chocolate with marshmallows?" Mother asks as she goes to the kitchen. There are jubilant cheers by small voices in answer to Mother's offer.

"I'll take that as a 'Yes Mother, please'," Mother called as she walked to the kitchen.

When Mother returns with the hot chocolate and we are sitting there looking at the tree, one of the smaller children always asks Father to tell them about Elmo the Elf and Sandy Clause. He would then tell us the story as it had been told to him by Elmo the Elf. Whenever he was asked to tell the story he would get a faraway look in his eyes. It was as if we children disap- peared and he was seeing it as it happened years ago. When the story was finished Father would sit in silence with a smile on his face, staring into the fire. Mother would qui- etly herd us children up the stairs and send us to bed and tuck us in.

On Christmas morning when we would rush down- stairs, there would be the tree sparking with lights and shiny ornaments. The tree was wrapped over, under, round and through with garlands of twisted foil, each branch dripping with cellophane icicles. I was always amazed that these icicles were always draped over the branches evenly spaced from deep in where the branch connected to the trunk to the very tip. The presents were all wrapped in colored paper and tied with fancy bows. They were piled high under the tree, spilling out and half filling the living room.

Someone, usually me, would look up from the presents and shout, "Look! Look at the mirror!" There written in a careful soap scroll would be Elmo's message.

MERRY CHRISTMAS & HAPPY NEW YEAR FROM SANDY CLAUSE and Elmo the ELF!

As I got older I asked Father to write the story down so I could tell the story of Elmo to my children. He told me that he had promised Elmo that he would tell the story to no one but family, and that he would not write it down till he was a hundred years old. Father passed away at 93 and I thought the story was lost forever, because after his passing the message was no longer written on the mirror.

Last year my father would have been a hundred years old. On Christmas morning when we came downstairs there was the tree all decorated, all sparking and beautiful. The presents cascaded out all over the living room floor. When we had opened all the presents and were relaxing, my daughter found a large brown envelope stuck in the back branches of the tree. She pulled it out and brought it to me.

"What's this?" she asked, "It says it's for you, Daddy!"

"For me? Let's see what is in it!"

I took the envelope and looked at the writing. It said, "FROM DAD." In the envelope was a leather-bound book. I slowly opened the book. On the first page was a single sentence: "My hundred years are up. Love, Dad."

I turned the next page and there I found this story written in my father's handwriting. I looked up from the book at my wife and children. It was then I glanced at the mirror behind them. I know it had not been there earlier, and I have no idea when or how it got there, but written on the mirror in soap was the message:

MERRY CHRISTMAS &
HAPPY NEW YEAR FROM
SANDY CLAUSE and Elmo
the Elf and Dad

I turned the page and began to read:

Our Meeting

I was living way up in the far north country. It was very early on Christmas morning when I was awakened from a sound sleep by something crashing down upon my cabin roof. My first thought was that a snow-heavy branch had broken away and fallen on the roof.

I decided that I would go up later and drag it off. I pulled the covers back up around my chin, and snuggled down nice and warm in my bed. I was just about to fall back to sleep when the moaning and groaning started. What in the world was making that noise? I tried to shut it out by ducking under the covers and stuffing the pillow in my ears, but I could still hear it.

"What in the world could be causing that noise?" I wondered.

It became obvious the noise was not going to stop and I couldn't sleep, so I threw off the covers and got out of bed. I got dressed as fast as I could. I stoked up the fire and added a log. The moaning and groaning sound was definitely coming down the chimney from the roof.

The cabin door was frozen shut. I pushed at it but it refused to budge. I backed away and rushed at the door hitting it with my shoulder.

The door flew open and I fell out head first into the snow. I lay there face down in the snow. I lay there, feeling the snow down my collar melt, listening. I could hear nothing. The noise had stopped. I had almost decided to get up and go back in the cabin. The noise, whatever it was, was gone. I got up and dusted the snow off and as I turned to go back into the cabin the moaning started again.

The morning was beautiful. The sun was just starting to peek over the edge of the land, chasing away the night's darkness as only the morning sunlight can. The snow was piled so high at the back of the cabin that I was able to walk right up onto the roof without a ladder. I climbed up to the peak of the roof and looked around. At first I saw nothing, then in a big mound of snow next to the chimney I saw a pair of size-four, green, pointy-toed shoes sticking out of the snow. I went over and tried to pull them out of the snow. To my surprise there were legs attached to the shoes. I dug away at the snow mound and was shocked to discover a twenty-two-inch tall elf frozen solid in a block of ice. The moaning and groaning continued but it was weaker now. I tried to pick him up so I could carry him down and thaw him out by the fire. Try as hard as I could, I could not move him, he was frozen solid to the roof. I ran down to the tool shed and gathered up some tools and returned to the roof. I banged with a shovel and pried with a pickaxe, but to no avail. Then very carefully I began to chip away at the ice with a wooden mallet and a chisel. He was moaning and groaning the whole time. By the time I broke him loose he was turning a deep blue. I grabbed him up, he was stiff as a board, I threw him over my shoulder and slipping and sliding I rushed down off the roof and into house to the fire inside the cabin.

I propped him up next to the fireplace, and threw on another log. As the fire began to roar he slowly began to melt. When he had thawed out a little I took off his little green hat and green jacket, dried him off, and put him on my bed and covered him up. It was when I took off his hat that I noticed that he had a lump on his head the size of a goose egg. I put some water on the stove to warm. My mother had always told me that hot water and duck fat was good for head bumps. I went to the pantry and got my can of duck fat. When the water had gotten warm enough I dropped in two heaping spoons full of the duck fat and watched it melt. When it had melted I dipped in a towel, wrung it out, and placed it on the bump on his head.

At the touch of the towel his eyes flew open. When they focused on me he did a double take.

"Oh my, oh me! What is this I see?"

He sat bolt upright in bed, looked to the left and to the right, then looking back at me he said, "Oh my! Oh me! You are a human! Why couldn't you be a dog, a cat, or even a flea?"

"I am a human as you can plainly see. I am not a dog a

cat or a flea. Why am I talking in rhyme?"

"When you talk to an elf,
speech comes out like that
most every time!"

"Who are you? How came
you to go *thud* on my roof?"

"I am Elmo, an elf, I fell
from a sleigh, thud on your
roof."

"What is an elf like you
doing on my roof? You fell
from a sleigh? What is this,
some spoof?"

"This is no spoof! When
elves have to speak to a
human they must tell the
truth."

"Elf, you say you fell from a sleigh on the ground going by! If you fell from a sleigh going by, how could you land upon my roof up high?"

"I fell from a sleigh, but not one on the ground. You see we were just sort of flying around."

"Flying around!? Not on the ground?! We! You mean there was someone else in a sleigh in the sky?"

"Yes, I was riding in a sleigh with a driver and his nine tiny reindeer, in the sky, sort of high."

"This person with whom you fly, does he wear a red suit, have a white beard and a twinkling eye?"

"Yes, he does. Now I suppose I must tell you the whole story of the Child, me, and Sandy, and how the very first Christmas came to be."

"Yes, that's a story I would like to hear!" Saying that I drew my chair up near.

Here, Son, I am writing the story, in his own words, exactly as Elmo the Elf told me it happened.

The Tale as Told by Elmo

It started a long time ago after dinosaurs and before radio. I was busy the day it started doing mischievous things, which was the elfin way. On the shepherd boys' tricks I did play.

When twilight came, the shepherds gathered their flocks and went down the hill to town. I could find nothing to do so I was just relaxing and sitting around. As I sat there watching the coming of night I noticed a star shining bright. I had never seen a star that had ever shown so bright. It showed near not from afar. Around it was a halo of golden light, like a crest. From the star came single silver shaft of light shown, down where it came to rest. It lit up the stable of the Bethlehem inn. I was curious, I just had to know what was going on within. Down the hill I crept as quiet as I could be. When I got to the stable I searched out a knothole through which I could have a look and see.

There were all kinds of humans standing in the dim stable light. There were wise men and shepherds standing off to the right.

Next to a manger, which was made of wood, a man named Joseph stood. His wife Mary knelt not far away looking at a boy child wrapped in swaddling clothes asleep in the hay. Around the Child's head a halo did glow as bright as the day.

"Who was this child?" I wondered. I just had to know.

Then through the knothole through which I did spy, I saw the beautiful Child open his eye. The Child looked straight at me and gave me a smile and a wink. That smile and wink made my elf heart sink.

I, as an elf, had never wanted to do anything for humans, but with that wink and that smile that night, I knew I wanted to do something for the Child that was wonderful and right. Then I knew what it was I must do, I turned and raced off into the night.

I would make toys for the Child, that's what I would do, but I guess I didn't really think the plan completely through.

I ran to my house under the old olive tree, and into my shop I did flee. I made balls of every size, color, and hue. Then I made wagons, one red, one blue. I made a doll that went *boo-hoo* and a stuffed owl that went *hoo,* but not *boo.* Then I made a clown that danced and bowed and said *How-de-do.* I made a yellow striped cat and some orange and blue kittens, and while I was at it, I knitted six pairs of red and green mittens. I made *whosit*s and *whatsi*ts and a bag that was for hitt'n'. I made a guitar that you strum and a big purple drum. I made a paddle with a rubber-band ball just for hitting. Little colored beanbags for throwing, and a big one for sitting. I made kites that you flew and horns that you blew. By the morning of the third day there were toys and stuff from the floor to the ceiling and, believe me, my poor head was reeling.

The sun was arising on the third day when I stuffed all the toys into a huge bag that was red. Then up the stairs and out the door, back to the stable I fled. I ran to the stable as quick as a wink, but when I got there I did not know what to think. I looked all around but there were no people to be found.

I didn't know what to think, there were quacking ducks and the chicken that went *cluck*. There was a cow at the trough taking a drink. The brown camel was there and the sheep with noses that were pink. When I couldn't find the Child, I felt my heart sink.

"Oh, where have they gone, does anyone know?"

"Oh they heard that the king wanted to hurt the Child, so they left on the fly!" said the goose. "They didn't even say a proper good-bye!"

"Why would anyone want to harm a beautiful Child such as he?" I asked, "Why couldn't they just leave him be?"

"Beats the heck out of me," shouted a flea.

"Where did they go? What did they say?"

"As I recall, they said that they were running away!" said a mouse from under the hay.

None of them knew or could point the way. I could find no other reason at the stable to stay. Back to my house under the old olive tree I fled. I sat down on the step my heart filled with dread, "Oh me, oh my," I started to cry.

"What seems to be amiss?" asked a voice that spoke with a hiss. "Why do you cry, little guy, you got something in your eye? Are your eyes sore?" It was the snake who lived under one of the big stable flag stones. The snake slithered up and coiled on the porch.

"No my eyes are not sore! I am crying because I am sad!" I raised my head and there sat the snake smiling. "Are you smiling to make me mad?"

"No, I've been smiling like this since I saw the Child!"

"You saw the Child!? Was that just now or back a while?"

"I saw the birth of the Child and since then I can't help but smile."

"I know," Elmo said, "he smiled and winked at me. But before I got back they had to flee. I made him all these toys, in this bag that you see. But I was too slow. Where did they go? Do you know?"

"Yes," hissed the snake, "they did seem in a hurry to leave. I can see how their departure would make you grieve."

"Did they say where they were going? Did they leave any clue? Did they say anything about where they were going to you?"

"Yes, I do believe that the donkey mentioned something when we spoke in his stall."

"Oh, tell me anything you remember anything at all!" I grabbed him up by the neck and shaking him said, "Tell me all you can recall!"

"Your grabbing does not help at all. Perhaps I could recall, if I had a biscuit, some tea and a soft place to coil."

"I'll get a pillow, and put on some tea to boil!" Dropping the snake, I said, "You wait here and rest your coil!"

Into my house I did dash. I slammed the teapot onto the stove with a crash. Of course, I filled it first with water at the sink. I grabbed the big yellow silk pillow, the one with tassels of pink. Back out I dashed, quick as a wink.

"Here, try this pillow it will help you, I think!"

"Ah, yes, this is ever so much better," said the snake as onto the pillow he did slink. "Oh, I do think my poor stomach is starting to shrink. Perhaps if I had a biscuit, a cup cake or pie and something cool to drink." I really didn't have time to think or to plan, back into the house I ran.

I grabbed up the chocolate cake with its gooey thick icing, and the tray of fudge I had set aside for dicing. I knew that the jellybeans would not go far, so I added some peanut brittle and licorice ropes to a big jar.

"There, that is all the goodies I own. Now with me don't play. What did you hear the donkey say?"

"Well, it seems that the king got jealous and wanted the Child slain. This, of course, filled the Child's parents with great anguish and pain. In a state of panic and dread the parents picked up the Child and fled. I can't remember what exact words were said, but for some reason the land of Egypt sticks in my head."

"Egypt!? Egypt!! I must follow, of course!" I ran into the house as quick as a flash. Into my pack clean and dirty cloths I did stash. Then putting on my great coat with its fur collar ruff and I tied the red sash and put on my ear-muff. Then throwing the red toy bag over my shoulder I started off in a dash. After three strides I stopped and came back.

"Good friend, snake, I'm not thinking this through. Where is this Egypt? Can you give me a clue?

"As I see it, you just pick any direction," said the snake with a grin. "If you are wrong, then you make a correction. You have four directions from which to choose. If you want to catch up you have no time to loose. If you pick the wrong one at first you have three others to choose, you can't lose! You could start by following the river. That would be a good start, I'd think. By the way, my good elf, in the stuff you leave, is there anything to eat or to drink?"

"Yes, there is water, tea, milk, and some soda that's pink. You can have it all, the furniture, the house, and the dirty dishes in the sink. I am off to Egypt—I think!"

"Thank you so much!" said the snake with a grin.

"Just follow the river as far as you can." Into the house he slithered, "I think that's the best plan."

"Good luck finding Egypt!" he hissed in a cold voice that would not melt butter, and with those final words he slammed the door and bolted the shutter.

My search for the Child turned out to be a major endeavor. It was destined to change my life forever. I walked many days across the land. Soon trees and grass gave way to hot desert sand. I was hot and thirsty and my red toy bag did drag.

Then as I staggered along I heard a voice that said. "Hey, kid! Whatcha got in the bag? What's in the sack? It looks like it's breaking your back."

I looked all around but there was nothing to see. There was nothing around but an old buzzard sitting high in a dead tree.

"Excuse me, sir. Were you talking to me?"

"Of course I was talking to you! You see anyone else around, but us two?" said the buzzard flying down to the ground.

"What you got in the bag, huh? What you got in the bag, huh?" The buzzard flapping his wings and hopping around did repeat, "I'll bet it is good stuff to eat, if I know my little boys."

"I am an elf, full grown, and not to be confused with little boys," I countered. "There is nothing to eat in my bag, it's only loaded with toys."

"Can you eat toys?"

"No!"

"Can you drink toys?"

"No!"

"If you can't eat toys, and you can't drink toys, what good are they?"

"I made them so that the Child would be happy and have something with which to play."

"What child is this?" asked the buzzard, licking his beak, "Is he fat and tender? Is he close by, this one that you seek?"

"I don't know! The last time I saw him he was not even a day old. He was being taken to Egypt by his parents, I was told."

"Egypt? Oh yeah, I know the place!" said the buzzard, his head buried deep in my pack looking for food.

"Egypt! You know where it is? Get out of my bag, Mister Buzzard, you are not only crude, but your also very, very rude."

"Ah, come on! I'm just looking for food."

"I'll give you a biscuit if you show me where this Egypt place is."

"For the promise of food, I'll answer any quiz! Yeah, I know this Egypt place, pyramids, sphinxes, and things like that. But I'll tell you, son, Egypt ain't no place to get fat, of course, every seven years or so they have a famine or drought. Man, that really helps the food situation out. During those times it's easy pick'ns. But with all that curry they use, it makes everything taste hot as the dickens. I'll tell you, I like the hot open desert where anything you find is cooked to a turn. Of course, if it sets too long it has a tendency to burn.

"Jungles ain't so bad, in the jungle there's all kinds of

food to be had. Jungles are regular delicatessen, there you can find not only meat, but salad with dress'n'. In the jungle I gain three sizes in the belly. All the food there is sorta like jelly. Everything there is soft and gushy. Everything there taste sorta like sushi."

"Well, that's all very interesting and I'd stay and visit, but I must be on my way. Now, here is your biscuit, take me to Egypt without delay!"

"Who is this kid who is wandering around by himself anyway?"

"I don't know his name," I cried, pushing the buzzard away with my boot, "he's not traveling alone. He is traveling with his mother and father and a donkey the color of soot."

"Oh, them! They passed by on this route!" said the buzzard. "I'll show you the way and maybe I'll find something to eat to boot."

First we walked and trudged across the southlands. Believe me when I tell you there is nothing in that desert but sun and sand. Then I went to the far, far, western land. I found nothing there that fit into my plan. There I stumbled and fumbled and for a while we followed a flock of wild geese. That is how we happened to search the far east. It was there we met a gopher who lived in a hole. He said that the Child and his parents might be at the North Pole. We decided that might be the way to go. We had walked north a fort-night when it started to snow, at first it was just here and there. Then before we knew what had happened, there was snow everywhere.

It was at this point that the buzzard began to brood. "You don't know how much I hate frozen food," he said. "This cold weather makes me fly funny. I'm going back where the weather is sunny, where the food is warm and runny."

Two days after the buzzard flew off it started to really snow. It fell so heavy that I could no longer tell which way to go. It snowed so hard that it didn't take the brain of a wizard for me to realize that I was caught in a blizzard. The sky was all white and everything around was white too. It was so cold that I began to turn blue. Onward I stumbled through the snow and the ice. I fell in deep snow banks not once but at lease twice. The second snow bank turned out to be not a bank at all. When I fell into the snow bank I fell through someone's door and into a hall. I lay there on the floor shivering and shaking with blue lips. When I looked up from the floor, over me stood a huge man with his hands on his hips. His hair and his beard were both curly and white, and the stump of a pipe was in his mouth clamped tight. He was ever so portly from shoulder to hip, as he looked down on me, a smile came to his lips.

"To whom do I address that lays on my hall floor? Who has come rushing, *crashing* through my door?"

"From the snow storm, sir, I could find no retreat, that is the reason I lay on your floor frozen at your feet!"

"There is no better place to hide from the storm you could have chosen. Come, my small friend, let us take you in and set you by the fire till you get unfrozen.

With that said he picked up my bag of toys in one hand and me in the other. He was a very strong man and the weight was no bother. Carrying me in, he kicked closed the door shutting out the cold air and set the toy bag down on the floor and me by the fire in a chair. He and his wife fed me hot chocolate and two bowls of hot vegetable soup. They covered me with soft flannel quilt, my eyelids started to droop. I hardly felt the man pick me up and carry me into the next room because I was so full and cuddly warm, I had fallen into a swoon.

I slept all that night and most of the next day. When I awoke I looked around the room, I was in dismay. There were toys everywhere I looked; it was quite a display. I hopped out of bed, got dressed and began looking around. I was amazed at what I found: there were toys everywhere, but most of them seemed broken.

From the next room I heard muffled words being

spoken. I went to the door and swung it wide open. There at the table sat the big man and his wife, they were talk'n' and jok'n'.

"Oh I'm glad to see you have finally awoken and got out of bed. You slept so long that we started to think you were dead."

"Yes, sit! Have some strawberry jam on my fresh baked bread," said the man's wife as into the kitchen she sped.

"Yes, please, sit, eat at our table," the big man said when his wife returned. "We want to hear your story as soon as you are able."

I told them of the star and what happened at the stable. I told of the Child and my toy-building spree. I told how the Child and his parents from the king had to flee. I told of my travels south, east and west, and how I had come to the North Pole following my quest.

"Kind sir and gracious madam," I said, "you have warmed me and bed me and now you have fed me. To you my thanks must be said. Thank you for your kindness.

I must admit that this is the first and only time I have conversed with humans with such ease. Could you tell me your names, please?"

"Oh, how thoughtless are we," said the big man after a pause. "This is my wife, Mary Noel, and I am Sanduscuis Tobusscus Clause, but most people who know me call me Sandy! Sandy Clause!"

Then the big man sat and holding the hand of his wife proceeded to tell me the story of his life.

"I was an actor at a tender young age. Throughout

Europe and Asia I was the rage. In Asia, I became entranced with its mysticism. It was there that I learned the ancient arts of disguise, illusion and hypnotism. Using these skills I could make an audience see what I wanted them to see. When I performed my stage name was Chris Kringle. In those days I always performed as a single. One day, while performing, I looked down into the front row and was smitten. There sat a beautiful young lady with the blue-green eyes of a kitten. Within a week into the marriage records we pledged our love and on her finger I placed a gold ring I got from a king. We stopped traveling and performing when Mother got sick. I tried mining for gold, but got over that quick. I couldn't stand being underground swinging a pick. I started collecting and selling antiques and bric-a-brac. Poor Mother, all day she would cough and she'd hack. I became very concerned about her condition. So I bundled her up and took her to a physician. He stuck a temperature stick in her mouth tight, while in her ears he showed a bright light. She kicked him real hard when with a rubber hammer he banged on her knee. He took a long time then he said, 'Madam, you have what is known as allergy.'

"I asked the doctor what was the cure? What could we do? The doctor said, 'Here is the advice that I have for you: You must go where there is no pollen, dust or trees. Go somewhere, where it is a con-stant zero degree.' So for that reason we moved to the

North Pole, away up here, where it is constantly cold.

"I started building our new house at the North Pole by digging a hole—that is when I discovered the gold. The gold made us rich beyond all our dreams. So we built this big house with its huge wooden beams. We also built a warehouse, a nursery, a hot house, a huge barn and two big warehouses. In the hot house we raise all our vegetables and fruit. In the barn we keep the ducks, pigs, cows, chickens, and sheep, and plenty of hay. In the stable is where the sleigh and nine reindeer stay. In my travels to gather materials I began to collect toys. I started by collecting the toys that children just threw aside and left unattended. Then I collected the ones that needed to be mended. Oh, I didn't take them the minute they were left, thrown aside and forgotten, on the ground. I would wait for a month or two for them to be found. I built one warehouse for the good toys and another larger one for the toys that were broken. You slept in the broken toy shop with the toys of which I have spoken."

"Yes," I said, "I saw them there. Why haven't they been mended?"

"It sad to say but my hands and fingers are so big I couldn't fix the toys as I intended!"

"I hate to brag, but I haven't seen a toy I couldn't fix!"

"Well, come on then and show me some of your tricks."

We went to the shop and I showed Sandy I wasn't jok'n', that I really could fix any toy that was broken. I fixed the toys and he painted, and as we worked we got better acquainted. Sandy and Mary Noel had wanted to have children a lot, as it turned out they could not. They had empty rooms all over the place. I told them that I couldn't help them with children but I could find elves to fill up the space. I told them I could provide elves of both genders and I told them of all the services an elf with reputation renders.

To the girl and women elves sewing, cooking, farming and housework were pure joys. The boy and men elves could do heavy work and help with the toys. We agreed that this was a good plan, so I sent out messages to every elf in the land. I told them that if they would stop causing the humans mischief and strife, they could come to the North Pole and live happily for the rest of their life. They came slowly at first then it was as if someone opened a dam. They flooded in till there wasn't an elf left any other place in the land. We became one big happy family, it was grand.

Then one day as I worked at my bench, I thought there was something important that I had forgotten to remember. Then it came to me that the Child's day of birth was the twenty-fifth of December. I ran to the calendar and there it was, in living black and white, the eve of the Child's birth was that night. I ran to my room and grabbed up the old red bag. Then I ran to the warehouse, I stuffed in toys till I made the old bag sag.

Sandy came to the warehouse and seeing me in a

frenzy, said, "Elmo, my friend, have you gone crazy? Have you lost your head?"

"Oh sir, it is my worst fear. Tomorrow is the Child's birthday and how I will find him is not clear."

"Do you know where to go? Is it far is it near?" Mary Noel did cry.

"As I said, I don't know but I must at least try."

Then Sandy laughed, "Ho! Ho! If you must do this then with you I'll go. I'll hook up the reindeer, walking will be way too slow. Get all the elves to pack the toys into the big sleigh tight. We can be ready to go by twilight tonight. But I fear, my friend, that the chances of finding your Child are very slight. I don't see how we can search the whole world in just one night. We might have a chance if we could fly like a meteor through the sky."

I stopped and let out a cry, "We can fly! Of course! We can fly! That is, if any of the elves have any Gigglefoogle leaves that are dry."

The Gigglefloogle plant is very, very rare. It only grows in the back of deep caves in the very high mountain air. When we elves find them we pick them and dry them with great care. We use these leaves to brew up a tea. If it is brewed right we can drink it and fly through the night at the speed of light. I asked all the elves to gather round and asked them to contribute all the leaves they had found. Among us we had enough leaves to brew up a big pot. But Sandy and I could fly, but the toys, which were not elfin or human, could not.

"I think you two are look-ing at this situation sort of

backward, boys" old Ezra elf said. "There is no way you two can carry all them toys. Them toys is all loaded and the reindeer is hitched to the sled. Feed the tea to them critters and you boys ride in the sleigh with the toys instead."

We arranged the reindeer two to each row except for the one whose nose had a glow. We put him in the lead; the light of his nose would guide us through the night.

Then we gave each of the reindeer a big drink of the brew. They at first stood very still, they didn't know exactly what to do. Then they began to react to the tea, they rose into the air and they flew. Up they went with the sleigh, the toys, Sandy, and me too.

We flew off that night to continue my quest. As the sun was setting Sandy turned the sleigh to the west. Whenever we got to a house, a hut, castle, or shack, we always followed the same line of attack. The reindeer would hover over the roof for a second or more while I dropped through the chimney and opened the door. Then Sandy would drag in the red bag full of toys. In each house I found sleeping children, both girls and boys. But the Child for whom I searched was not found so onward we flew.

After each house the toy bag seemed to get light so I would stuff in more toys as we sped through the night. We searched every place that people could live, because we had presents for the Child to give. Search as we might, the results were the same—land, drag the red bag in, find nothing—it was always the same. It all started to feel like a hide-

and-seek game. At each house when we did not find the Child we felt our chances decrease. We were very discouraged as we started to search the houses in the east.

We had searched all the houses west, north, and south, as we turned for home our spirits were down in the mouth. As the morning sun was just reaching the earth's crest I saw a small house off in the west. We flew to this little house and I dropped down the chimney as quiet as a mouse. As out of the fireplace hearth I crawled I looked around and stood enthralled. There in the living room stood a small evergreen tree. It was the prettiest thing that you ever wanted to see. It was covered with candles from the top to the ground, white and colored popcorn garlands were wrapped round and round. On the top a silver star rested like a crown, glittering beads and bobbles from every limb hung down.

Then from a crib that I had failed to see came a voice. "Hello elf! Are you looking for me?"

I rushed to the crib and there sat the Child, I busted out laughing with glee.

"Oh my goodness, it is really you, all my hopes and dreams have come true. You cannot imagine what I have brought you."   .

Then I heard a light tapping at the door, I had forgotten poor Sandy outside. I ran to it and threw it open wide.

"Look, I found him at last! Hurry, bring all of the toys inside!"

Sandy stood at the door, he looked like he was about to

cry. He held out the big red bag and then said with a sigh:

"There are no more toys in the sleigh and the bag is empty too. There is a hole in the bag that I fear they fell through."

I snatched the red bag out his hand and looked at the bag, what he said was true. "Oh! This is just grand! It looks like our mission is a bust, we are through! We dragged the toy bag from house to house all over this land. Whatever went wrong with our careful plan?"

"I do not believe that the cause of our failing was you or me," said Sandy. "The bag's got a hole in it from dragging it, don't you see?"

"We have come oh so far only to fail," I cried with a wail. "At each house we stopped at, we must have left a toy trail."

"After each house we had to fill the bag back up to the brim. I should have realized that something was not right," Sandy said, "Boy, am I dim!"

I turned to the Child and said, "I am so sorry! I don't

know what to say. We had so much to give you and it has been lost on the way."

"Come on, Elmo!" implored Sandy. "We'll just return and pick up the toys, for Heaven's sake! We've got to hurry before the children awake."

"No! We can't, don't you see? There's not enough time and the reindeer are out of tea."

"Stay!" said the Child. "My parents decorated this tree to celebrate my birth date. But what you two have done I think is first rate. By dragging your big red toy bag to every house in the land I think you were just following our Father's plan. I shall grow up and in time I shall leave this life. You two and yours will live forever through all the world's strife. On my birthday each year you will bring good cheer and joy and, of course, the toys. To the adults you will bring peace and happiness, and to all children you will bring great toys. For this one short day each year, for a few happy moments it will be remembered that I was alive, and through you, the memory of me will survive. Through you, Elmo the Elf and Sandy Clause, belief in me on this day will never die!"

Saying that, Elmo hopped off the stool where he sat. "So, I have told you the tale of how Christmas came to be! Now, my friend, I must take my leave and flee! Thank you for the warmth of your fire and the hot chocolate, good cheer and tender care! But now I must get out of here and meet my friend out there."

Before I could move or speak he was out the door, as fast as a cat he did streak. I heard sleigh-bells, laughter, and hooves prancing on my snowy front lawn. By the time I got into my coat and outside, they were gone. But I heard them exclaim as they disappeared into the new dawn's light.

MERRY CHRISTMAS TO ALL & MAY ALL YOUR FUTURES BE BRIGHT!

The End
DAD

Printed in the United States
6587

9 781587 361005